Tatty Ratty

For Pandora

TATTY RATTY

A CORGI BOOK 0 552 54630 5

First published in Great Britain by Doubleday,
an imprint of Random House Children's Books

Doubleday edition published 2001
Corgi edition published 2002

1 3 5 7 9 10 8 6 4 2

Copyright © Helen Cooper 2001
Designed by Ian Butterworth

Corgi Books are published by Random House
Children's Books,
61-63 Uxbridge Road, London W5 5SA,
a division of The Random House Group Ltd,
in Australia by Random House Australia (Pty) Ltd,
20 Alfred Street, Milsons Point, Sydney, NSW 2061,
Australia,
in New Zealand by Random House New Zealand Ltd,
18 Poland Road, Glenfield, Auckland 10, New Zealand,
and in South Africa by Random House (Pty) Ltd,
Endulini, 5A Jubilee Road, Parktown 2193, South Africa

THE RANDOM HOUSE GROUP
Limited Reg. No. 954009
www.kidsatrandomhouse.co.uk

A CIP catalogue record for this book is available
from the British Library.

Printed in Singapore by Tien Wah Press [PTE] Ltd

Tatty Ratty

Helen Cooper

London

New York

Sydney

Picture Corgi Books

Tatty-Ratty was lost.
"When did you see him last?"
said Mum.
"In the kitchen," sniffed Molly.
"And then on the bus."
"And after the bus?" groaned Mum.
"I don't know," sobbed Molly.

"Let's look for him," said Mum.
So they went and looked in the usual places,
the sort of places they'd found him before.
Under the sofa, behind the bin,
but they couldn't see a whisker or paw of him.

Mum called the bus company.
"No, we haven't found anything yet,"
said the man on the phone.
"What are we going to do?" wailed Molly.
"I can't sleep without Tatty-Ratty."

"You can sleep with us, so you won't
be lonely," said Dad.
"Tatty-Ratty'll be lonely on the bus,"
worried Molly.

"Maybe he'll hop off,"

whispered Dad.

"He might," said Molly, snuggling down.
"He'll find a train and drive it home."
"Will he wear a uniform?" murmured Dad.

"Not a whole uniform," Molly yawned.
"When I first got him, he had blue buttons.
That's all he'll need."

"Tatty-Ratty's driving a train,"
Dad told Mum the next morning.

"Not any more," said Molly.
"He's having porridge
with the Three Bears.
He's eating... and eating...
and getting fat."

But that night, at bath time, Molly said,

"I want Tatty-Ratty."

"Isn't he with the Three Bears?" said Mum.

"Not any more," said Molly.

"He ate so much his stuffing hurt.

Now he's coming home, with Cinderella."

"Mmmm," said Mum. "She'll clean him up,

she'll mend all his holes, and brush his fur."

"He won't like it,"

warned Molly.

Molly knew what Tatty-Ratty
would do. He'd bite Cinderella,
if she brushed his fur.
He'd scrabble, and scuttle
right through the window,
and bounce down a mountain,
into the sea.

She told Mum what would happen.

"What a bad rabbit," said Mum.
"Well, at least he'll be clean. But I hope he can swim."

Molly said,
"Pirates will save him.
He'll sail on their boat,
and peep at their treasure,
and sneak a look at their secret map,
and then...
he'll know the way home."

It was time for bed,
but Molly said,
"I won't sleep without
Tatty-Ratty."
"He's busy reading that map,"
said Mum.
"Not any more," said Molly.

"The pirates didn't like
sharing their map, so they

strung

him

up

by

the

bunny

ears!"

"He'll find a way to escape,"
said Mum. "He always does."

"A dragon will save him," said Dad.

"It'll swoop down, just like this...

...and lift Tatty-Ratty like this..."

Molly yelled, "He'll be cold in the sky."

"He'll grow more fur," said Dad.

Molly growled, "Will he come home on the dragon?"

"Not when you're making that noise," said Dad.

"Dragons like peace and quiet."

"So where will they go?" said Molly.

"They'll fly to the moon,"

said Dad.

"And will the Man in the Moon
be there?"

"Oh, indeed he will," said Dad.
"He'll roll Tatty-Ratty
in moon dust,
till his fur turns sugary white."

"He'll like that," murmured Molly.

Molly dreamed of a spaceship.
It belonged to the
Man in the Moon.
And it zoomed across the sky,
with Tatty-Ratty riding inside.

The spaceship hovered over Molly's town,
and Tatty-Ratty bailed out.
Soon he drifted down...

...and down...
But before he landed,
Molly woke.

Molly told Mum her dream.
"That means he's almost home," sighed Mum.
"If you close your eyes and go to sleep,
we'll find him when the sun comes up."

The sun came up very early.

"I'm sure he's somewhere
here," yawned Mum.
"Remember, he might look
different," yawned Dad.
"Yes, he'll be wearing his buttons,"
said Molly.
"And all that porridge
will've made him fat."
"He'll be very clean and fluffy,"
smiled Mum.
"I know," said Molly,
"but he'll still be Tatty-Ratty."

Kingdom
of
Bunny

OPEN
7-TILL-
MIDNIGHT

Kingdom
of

There were a lot of rabbits.
"What about this one?" said Dad.

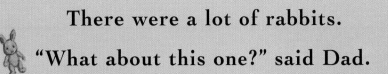

"That's not Tatty-Ratty," said Molly.

"Maybe this one?" said Mum.
"Don't be silly," said Molly.

"Look!" shouted Molly.

"He's pricking his ears, and he's lovely and white."

"He's smiling at me!"

"About time too,"

whispered Tatty-Ratty.